FRED BEAR and FRIENDS

Copyright © ticktock Entertainment Ltd 2007
First published in Great Britain in 2007 by ticktock Media Ltd.,
Unit 2, Orchard Business Centre, North Farm Road,
Tunbridge Wells, Kent, TN2 3XF

author: Melanie Joyce
ticktock project editor: Julia Adams
ticktock project designer: Emma Randall
ticktock image co-ordinator: Lizzie Knowles

We would like to thank: Colin Beer, Tim Bones, James Powell, Rebecca Clunes,
Dr. Naima Browne, Victoria Eaton and the staff at StoneRock Dental Care Hawkhurst and Graham Knowles

ISBN 978 1 84696 504 3 pbk

Printed in China

Picture credits
All photography by Colin Beer of JL Allwork Photography except for the following: Shutterstock: 24.

Every effort has been made to trace the copyright holders, and we apologise in advance for any unintentional omissions.
We would be pleas   edition of this publication.

Meet Fred Bear and Friends

Fred

Arthur

Betty

Also starring...

Jess

Anna

Roger

Ben

Lucy

Today, Fred and Jess are going to the dentist.

Jess is excited. She has never been to the dentist before.

Fred and Jess brush their teeth before they go to the dentist.

When Fred and Jess arrive at the dentist, they find a seat in the waiting room.

They meet some of their friends there, too.

"Why do we go to the dentist?" asks Jess.

"So our teeth stay healthy and strong," says Fred.

The waiting room is fun.
There are toys to play with.

Fred helps Jess read a book.

Roger and Anna play with
their favourite toy.

Lucy and Ben do a puzzle.

"Fred Bear and
Jess, please."
says the
dental nurse.

"Let's go, it's our
turn," says Fred.

They follow the
dental nurse
into the surgery.

"Come in,"
says the dentist.

The surgery is very
bright and clean.

Jess spots the
dentist's chair:
"Wow!"

says Jess. "Look
at the big chair."

"I will go first,"
says Fred.
"Then you will
know what happens."

Fred climbs onto
the big chair.

The dentist puts on soft gloves and a mask.

"Click,"

goes a big light.

"This helps me see Fred's teeth," says the dentist. "Open wide, Fred!"

Fred's teeth look very healthy today.

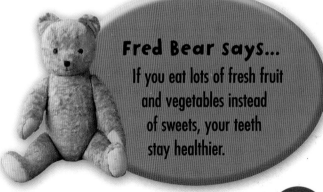

Fred Bear says...
If you eat lots of fresh fruit and vegetables instead of sweets, your teeth stay healthier.

Now it is Jess' turn. Her teeth are very healthy. They just need a clean.

'**Zzzzz,**' goes the polishing brush.

The dentist uses these things, too:

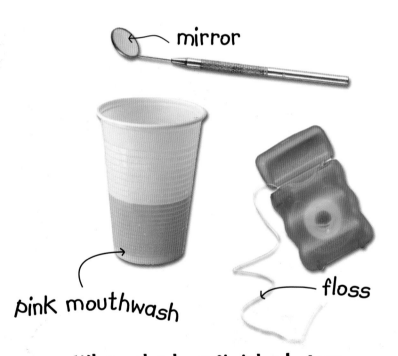

mirror

pink mouthwash

floss

When she has finished, Jess rinses her mouth with the tasty pink mouthwash.

Fred and Jess get a lovely sticker when they are both finished.

"Remember to brush your teeth in the morning and at bedtime," says the dentist. "And don't eat too many sweets. They are not good for your teeth."

Fred and Jess say "Goodbye" to the dentist.

The receptionist gives Fred and Jess a card each. These tell them when their next visit will be. They have to come back in 6 months, on 12th June.

Fred shows Jess where June is on the calendar.

"Goodbye! See you next time," says Jess.

At home, Jess pretends
to be a dentist.
She puts on a mask
like the real dentist.

"Open wide,"
she says to Betty.

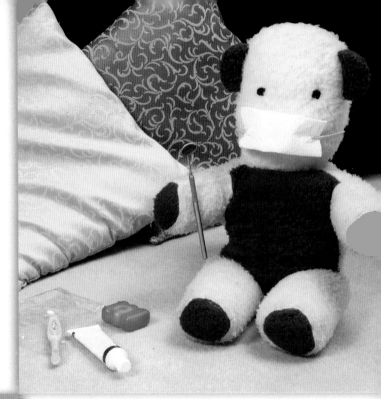

Then it is Arthur's turn.
"Let's see if your teeth
are nice and clean,"
says Jess.

Jess likes being
a dentist!

Keeping your teeth healthy

There are many different things that help keep your teeth healthy. Can you match these things to the questions on the next page?

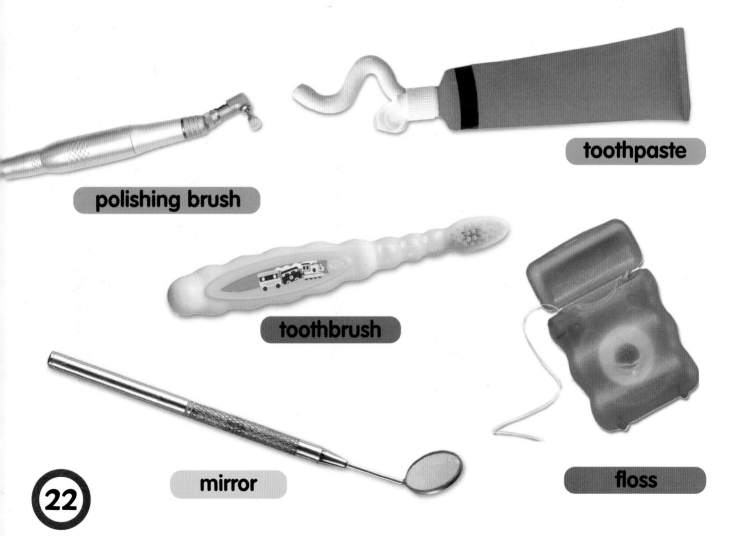

polishing brush

toothpaste

toothbrush

floss

mirror

Jess uses three things to keep her teeth clean. What are they?

The dentist polishes Jess' teeth. This makes them very clean. What does he use?

The dentist checks Jess' teeth to see if they are healthy. What does he use to see inside Jess' mouth?

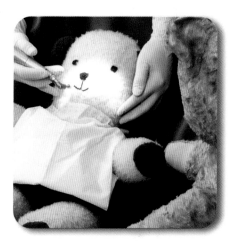

23

Healthy food

Look at these pictures. What is good and what is bad for your teeth?